First published in Great Britain 1986 by Blackie and Son Ltd

British Library Cataloguing in Publication Data
Hayes, Barbara
Annabel Visits the Country.—(A Town and Country Mouse Story)
I. Title II. Mendoza, Phillip III. Series
813′.54[J] PZ7

ISBN 0 216 92030 2

Blackie and Son Limited
7 Leicester Place
London WC2H 7BP

Printed in Belgium

Annabel Visits the Country

Barbara Hayes
Illustrated by Phillip Mendoza

Blackie

Chug-a-puff! Chug-a-puff! Flora and Fred were waiting at the station. Cousin Annabel was coming on her very first visit to the country.

"Here she is!" said Flora, waving with great excitement as Annabel stepped on to the platform, followed by a huge pile of luggage.

"How lovely to see you both," cried Annabel, rushing up and giving Flora and Fred each a big hug. "Now, where's the taxi?"

"There are no taxis in the country," laughed Flora. "But Fred will push your luggage in his cart."

"No taxis!" gasped Annabel. "How do we get home?"

"We walk, of course," said Flora. "Don't worry. It will only take an hour . . ."

"I'm sure you would like a bath after your long journey," said Flora to Annabel when they reached her little cottage. "If you want to go to your room and unpack I'll get it ready."

When Annabel had finally finished unpacking all her suitcases she came downstairs.

"Where's the bath?" she asked.

"Here, in front of the fire," said Flora. "You wouldn't want to have a bath outside, would you?"

"How quaint!" gasped Annabel, rather faintly.

After supper Annabel went upstairs to change. She felt sure they would go out for the evening.

"I'll think I'll change, too," yawned Flora.

But while Annabel was putting on her party clothes, Flora was putting on her nightdress. "Goodnight, Annabel," said Flora, sleepily. "I do like your dressing gown."

Next morning Annabel cheered up when Flora said they must go out. Annabel thought they were going shopping, but they only went outside the back door to pick beans from the garden!

Just then, Fred passed by on his bicycle. "Come to the farm and help with the harvest," he said.

But that was even worse. Harvesting was all hard work and prickles!

"How dull the countryside is," Annabel thought, and she decided to write to her friend Jeremy to ask him to come and take her home.

But no sooner had she posted her letter than something very exciting happened! Mr Badger the postman delivered a letter from Australia!

"It's from Cousin Bruce," cried Flora. "He's coming to see us. He said to meet him at the crossroads at 10 o'clock on Tuesday."

'That's today!" squeaked Annabel.

They hurried off to the crossroads just in time to see Cousin Bruce pulling up in his big shiny car. Flora and Annabel were thrilled to meet their Australian cousin and soon all three were chatting like old friends.

"I've come to solve a mystery," Bruce explained. "Many years ago my grandfather lived here. When he went to Australia he left behind an old box — full of treasure!"

"Oooh," squeaked Annabel. "Where is it?"

"That's the mystery," said Bruce. "Grandpa gave me this map and this clue. It's all he could remember." He read out the clue:

Over the gurgles, there's the box,
Through the hatch of the house with the thatch.

Suddenly Flora squealed, "But that's where Great Aunt Sarah lives — in her thatched cottage!"

Off they all went at once to see Great Aunt Sarah.

"I know nothing about any treasure," said Great Aunt Sarah when they told her all about it. "But you're welcome to have a look."

"Now where could the gurgles be?" asked Bruce.

"We'll never find the gurgles," said Annabel, and she turned on the tap to get herself a drink.

Just then everyone heard a loud gurgling sound — it came from the roof.

"Of course!" said Bruce. "The water tank! Up in the attic! That's what 'through the hatch' means."

Sure enough, over the gurgling water tank lay a dusty old linen box filled with gold pieces! But what should they do with it all?

In the end they decided to give the treasure to Great Aunt Sarah. After all, it was her house.

After all the excitement Annabel was much more cheerful. "I shall go horse riding," she announced.

"You'll have to ride old Buttercup," said Flora. "He's the only horse in the village."

Old Buttercup was so large and wobbled so much, Annabel could hardly stay on him. And when he began to gallop, she couldn't stay on at all!

"Oh! *Where* is Jeremy?" she wailed when she fell off for the third time.

In fact, Jeremy wasn't far away. But his nice new car had broken down just outside the village.

Mendoza

In the end, Fred had to tow Jeremy and Annabel home behind his muddy old tractor. How embarrassed Annabel was!

"I never want to see another green field again," she said. "Town mice should stay in the town!"

The next day the postman brought Flora a parcel. It was a pretty thank-you present from Annabel. "How nice," said Flora, holding up the present. "I'm sure Annabel can't wait to visit us again — I must invite her back soon."